Paul Friester was born in 1961 in Kapfenberg, Austria. He has lived in Vienna since the eighties, working as a freelance writer. His stories about the little owl have become international bestsellers.

Philippe Goossens was born in 1963 in Brussels, where he still lives with his family. Since graduating from the Institut Saint-Luc, Philippe Goossens has worked as a freelance illustrator and has already illustrated more than fifty books for children and young people.

Copyright © 2016 by NordSüd Verlag AG, CH-8005 Zürich, Switzerland.
First published in Switzerland under the title *Heule Eule - Ich will mein BUMM!*
English translation copyright © 2016 by NorthSouth Books Inc., New York 10016.
English translation by Erica Stenfalt.

First published in the United States, Great Britain, Canada, Australia, and New Zealand in 2016 by NorthSouth Books Inc., an imprint of NordSüd Verlag AG, CH-8005 Zürich, Switzerland.
Distributed in the United States by NorthSouth Books Inc., New York 10016.
Library of Congress Cataloging-in-Publication Data is available.
Printed in Germany by Grafisches Centrum Cuno GmbH & Co. KG, Calbe, October 2015.
ISBN: 978-0-7358-4246-5 (trade)
1 3 5 7 9 • 10 8 6 4 2

www.northsouth.com

Paul Friester ◈ Philippe Goossens

Owl Howl
and the
BLU-BLU

North South

One day, Little Owl was waiting for her mommy and gazing up at the sky.

She saw a beautiful BLU-BLU
floating by.
But suddenly it was gone.

Puzzled, Little Owl looked all around.
Where did it go?
And then she started to howl:
"HOO-HOO-
HOOO!!!"
Really loud.

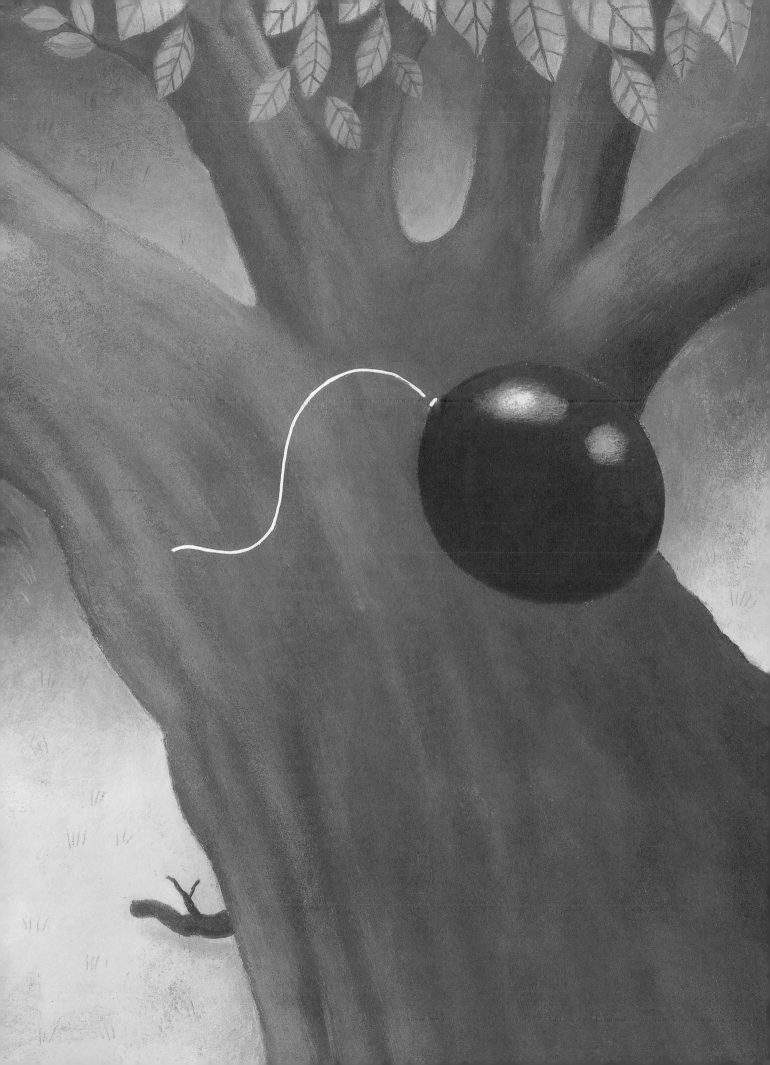

Startled, the hedgehog stuck his nose out of his bed of leaves and asked, "Good heavens! What's wrong?"
"It's gone!" sniffed the little owl.

"How? What? Who is gone?" asked
Mrs. Squirrel, confused.
"The BLU-BLU!" sobbed the baby
owl. "HOO-HOO-HOOO!!!"
"What's a BLU-BLU?" wondered
Mrs. Squirrel.

"BLU-BLU sounds like something to eat," suggested the mole.
"Little Owl probably lost a piece of candy. Or some buttery, yellow popcorn."
"No, HOO-HOOO!" cried the baby owl. "My BLU-BLU is red!"

"Red? I've got it!" declared the
mole happily. "She wants to play cards!"
He fetched a red box from his hole and
announced, "Okay, the game is called Ready
Steady Boom, and this is what you do. . . ."

"No, no, HOO-HOOO!" howled Little Owl.
"My BLU-BLU is round, not a rectangle!"

The old stag beetle scuttled along next.

"Shhh! What's all this noise?" he scolded.

"I want my BLU-BLU!" howled Little Owl. "HOO-HOOO!"

"Tut, tut! When you grow into a big owl, you'll learn that you can't always have what you want," said the stag beetle sternly.

"But I'm not a big owl!" cried Little Owl. "I'm a little owl. And I want my BLU-BLU! And when I want something, I really, really want it! HOO-HOO-HOOO!"

"Oh dear, I'm afraid that's true," sighed Mommy Owl, who had just arrived back. "But I know what Little Owl wants. It's red and round . . ."

"Of course, she wants a ball!" exclaimed the stag beetle. Quickly, he rolled over a big ball of dung and muttered, "There you go. I just got this ball from my cousin, the dung beetle. It's brown and doesn't smell so good, but you can still play with it. Just stop howling!"

"No, no, no, no!" screeched Little Owl.
"My BLU-BLU doesn't smell bad, and anyway, it can fly!
HOO-HOO-HOOO!"

Just then the crow stopped by and asked,
"CAW! What's wrong with her today?"
The hedgehog, the squirrel, and the mole held
their noses as they explained the problem.

"It's red, round, and can fly?" repeated the crow
thoughtfully. "I think I just saw something like that.
Come with me!"
Bursting with curiosity, they all ran, scuttled, or flew
along behind the crow.
When they reached the old oak tree, the crow
pointed upward and asked, "Is that it?"

"YESSS!" squealed Little Owl with delight. She flew up into the tree and started poking the balloon.
"NOOOO!" shrieked all the animals, covering their ears.
But Little Owl hollered gleefully:

"Ready . . .

steady . . .

And then Little Owl fluttered back down to her forest friends and begged, **"Again! Again!"**